'Aqeedah & Fiqh

WORK BOOK

ADAPTED FROM THE

SAUDI CURRICULUM

First Edition: 2008
Second Edition: 2010
ISBN 978-1-60585-925-5

Translator & Compiler: Umm 'Abdis Salaam Al Grenaadiyyah

Published & Distributed by: Salafy Ink Publications
Visit us on the web at www.salafyink.com
Email: salafyink@gmail.com

Editing & Typesetting: Proof 2 Print
Email: proof2print@gmail.com

Cover Design: Usul Concept & Design
(www.usuldesign.com)

Available online and in book stores

Salafy Ink
PUBLICATIONS

Table of Contents

Introduction	3
What is Tawheed?	9
Review Questions	13
The five Pillars of Islaam	15
Review Questions	21
The Six articles of Faith	25
Review Questions	27
Ihsan	29
Review Questions	30
Shurooyus Salaat	31
Review Questions	36
The Wudu	40
Review Questions	42
The things that Nullify the Wudu	43
Review Questions	44
The Shuroot of the Wudu	46
Review Questions	48
Arkaanus Salaat	50
Review Questions	54
Puzzle Tawheed and Fiqh	57
Test Prep	59

Introduction

Indeed all praise is due to Allah; we praise Him and seek His aid and forgiveness. And we seek refuge with Allah from the evils of ourselves and from the evil of our actions. Whosoever Allah guides, there is no misguidance for him. And whosoever Allah leads astray, there is no guidance for him. And I testify that there is nothing worthy of worship except Allah and that Muhammad is His servant and Messenger.

يَاأَيُّهَا الَّذِينَ ءامَنُوا اتَّقُوا اللهَ حَقَّ تُقَاتِهِ وَلا تَمُوتُنَّ إِلا وَأَنتُم مُسلِمُونَ

"O you who believe! Fear Allah as He should be feared, and do not die except in a state of Islaam." [Aali 'Imraan: 102]

يَاأَيُّهَا النَّاسُ اتَّقُوا رَبَّكُمُ الَّذِي خَلَقَكُم مِن نَفسٍ وَاحِدَةٍ وَخَلَقَ مِنْهَا زَوجَهَا وَبَثَّ مِنهُمَا رِجَالا كَثِيرًا وَنِسَاءً وَاتَّقُوا اللهَ الَّذِي تَسَاءلُونَ بِهِ وَالأَرحَامَ إِنَّ اللهَ كَانَ عَلَيكُم رَقِيبًا

"O Mankind! Fear your Lord who has created you from a single soul and from him created his spouse, and from them He created many men and women. Fear Allah through Whom you demand your mutual rights and do not cut the ties of kinship, for surely Allah is ever an All Watcher over you!" [Surah An Nisaa: 1]

يَاأَيُّهَا الَّذِينَ ءامَنُوا اتَّقُوا اللهَ وَقُولُوا قَولا سَدِيدًا، يُصلِح لَكُم أَعمَالَكُم وَيَغفِر لَكُم ذُنُوبَكُم وَمَن يُطِعِ اللهَ وَرَسُولَهُ فَقَد فَازَ فَوزًا عَظِيمًا

"O you who believe! Fear Allah and say truthful speech, He will direct you to righteous deeds and forgive your sins. And whosoever obeys Allah and His Messenger, he has indeed achieved a great achievement." [Surah Al Ahzaab: 70-71]

Indeed the best of speech is the Book of Allah and the best of guidance is the guidance of Muhammad. And the worst of affairs are newly invented matters, and every newly invented matter is an innovation and every innovation is a misguidance and every misguidance is in the hellfire. To proceed…

It is a right of the Muslim child that their parents strive to educate and teach them the sound Islaamic creed. Allah says in His Noble Book,

وَإِذْ قَالَ لُقْمَانُ لِابْنِهِ وَهُوَ يَعِظُهُ يَا بُنَيَّ لَا تُشْرِكْ بِاللَّهِ إِنَّ الشِّرْكَ لَظُلْمٌ عَظِيمٌ

"And (remember) when Luqman said to his son when he was advising him: "O my son! Join not in worship others with Allah. Verily! Joining others in worship with Allah is a great wrong indeed." [Surah Luqman: 13]

It is also the right of the child that their parents protect them from that which will harm them; whether that harm be potential, temporary or ultimate, Allah says,

يَا أَيُّهَا الَّذِينَ آمَنُوا قُوا أَنفُسَكُمْ وَأَهْلِيكُمْ نَارًا وَقُودُهَا النَّاسُ وَالْحِجَارَةُ عَلَيْهَا مَلَائِكَةٌ غِلَاظٌ شِدَادٌ لَا يَعْصُونَ اللَّهَ مَا أَمَرَهُمْ وَيَفْعَلُونَ مَا يُؤْمَرُونَ

"O you who believe! Ward off from yourselves and your families a Fire (Hell) whose fuel is men and stones, over which are (appointed) angels stern (and) severe, who disobey not, (from executing) the

Commands they receive from Allah, but do that which they are commanded." [Surah At Tahrim: 6]

Keeping this in mind one can determine that a sound and firm upbringing upon the proper Islaamic creed while acting upon it, will undoubtedly assist them in the attainment of ultimate success and escape from ultimate harm, Allah says,

كُلُّ نَفْسٍ ذَآئِقَةُ الْمَوْتِ وَإِنَّمَا تُوَفَّوْنَ أُجُورَكُمْ يَوْمَ الْقِيَامَةِ فَمَن زُحْزِحَ عَنِ النَّارِ وَأُدْخِلَ الْجَنَّةَ فَقَدْ فَازَ وَما الْحَيَاةُ الدُّنْيَا إِلاَّ مَتَاعُ الْغُرُورِ

"Everyone shall taste death. And only on the Day of Resurrection shall you be paid your wages in full. And whoever is removed away from the Fire and admitted to Paradise, he indeed is successful. The life of this world is only the enjoyment of deception (a deceiving thing)." [Surah Aali 'Imran: 185]

Knowing that we will all die, be resurrected and judged for the actions that we put forth, we must then by default acknowledge the fact that beneficial knowledge must precede beliefs, statements and actions. In fact, righteous actions are only built upon beneficial knowledge. Thus the proper Islaamic Education (i.e. beneficial knowledge) should constantly be a concern and on the mind of every single individual, and in particular parents and educators.

We advise both the father and the mother to strive hard in educating their children and teaching them the Book of Allah and the Sunnah of His messenger *(SallAllahu alaihi wa sallam)*. They must also set a living example for their children; showing them by way of their actions the methodology of the Salaf (the Pious Predecessors *(radi Allahu 'anhum)*. The parents should be close to their children, meaning, they should not leave them for long periods of time, unaware of their actions. They should know those things that their children deem important. They should always strive to safeguard and protect their children. They should be vigilant and aware of their children's situations, conditions, comings and goings etc. They should also pay attention and if necessary reprimand their children so that their statements and actions conform to the Islaamic legislation and Sunnah of the Prophet *(SallAllahu alaihi wa sallam)*. A servant must fear Allah with regards to their children and not feed (clothe or house) them except from that which is Halaal (permissible). (Lastly), the parents must purify their intentions and even before they try to have children, they should intend to have offspring whom they would teach the truth, so that they in turn can spread it to the rest of creation.

O dear reader what you have between your hands is the first of a series of educational books based on and adapted from the Saudi curriculum. We hope that all concerned educators and homeschool instructors can find use for this book and thus utilize it in the proper Islaamic Education of their children, so that -by Allah's Will- they may attain the great success.

We ask that Allah make this work solely for His Sake, beneficial to us and the rest of His creation, and heavy in our scale of good deeds, verily Allah is over all things capable.

Abu 'Abdis Salaam Siddiq Al Juyaanee

❀ ❀ ❀

What is Tawheed?

Tawheed is the singling out of Allah alone with all worship. It is the religion of the Prophets that Allah sent to teach mankind.

Allah says,

وَلَقَدْ بَعَثْنَا فِي كُلِّ أُمَّةٍ رَّسُولاً أَنِ اعْبُدُواْ اللّهَ وَاجْتَنِبُواْ الطَّاغُوتَ

"And verily, We have sent among every Ummah (community, nation) a Messenger (proclaiming): Worship Allah (alone) and avoid (or keep away from) Taghut (all false deities)" [Surah An Nahl: 36]

Categories of Tawheed

There are three categories of Tawheed.

1. Tawheed Ar Ruboobiyyah (The Oneness of Allah's Lordship).

2. Tawheed Al Uloohiyyah (The Oneness of the worship of Allah).

3. Tawheed Al Asma wa Siffat (The Oneness of the Names and Attributes of Allah).

The three categories of Tawheed can be found in the Qur'an. The proof for the three categories are,

Allah's saying,

بِسْمِ اللّٰهِ الرَّحْمَنِ الرَّحِيمِ

"In the name of Allah, the Most Beneficent, the Most Merciful." [Surah al Fatihah: 1]

And also His saying,

رَبُّ السَّمَاوَاتِ وَالْأَرْضِ وَمَا بَيْنَهُمَا فَاعْبُدْهُ وَاصْطَبِرْ لِعِبَادَتِهِ هَلْ تَعْلَمُ لَهُ سَمِيًّا

"Lord of the heavens and the earth and whatever is between them, so worship Him (alone) and be constant and patient in His worship. Do you know of any who is similar to Him? (Of course none is similar or coequal or comparable to him, and He has none as a partner with Him). [There is nothing like unto Him and He is the All Hearer, the All Seer]." [Surah Maryam: 65]

Tawheed Ar Ruboobiyyah

This is to believe in the Oneness of Allah's Lordship. To believe that Allah is the Creator, the One who provides, the Causer of life and death, and other than that from Lordship.

The proof of this is Allah's saying,

الْحَمْدُ لِلَّهِ رَبِّ الْعَالَمِينَ

"All praise and thanks belong to Allah the Lord of the Alamin (all that exists, mankind and jinn)." [Surah Al Fatihah: 2]

Tawheed Al Uloohiyyah

This is to believe that Allah is deserving of all worship and that nothing else should be worshiped along with him. All acts of worship are done solely for Allah. A Muslim's salaat (prayer), du'ah (supplication), slaughtering (of animals), seeking forgiveness, love, hope, fear, and other than that are from acts of worship.

Allah says,

وَمَا خَلَقْتُ الْجِنَّ وَالْإِنسَ إِلَّا لِيَعْبُدُونِ

"And I did not create the Jinn and Mankind except to worship Me (alone)." [Surah Adh Dhariyyat: 56]

Tawheed Al Asma wa Siffat

This is to believe in the oneness of Allah's Names and Attributes. To affirm all of Allah's Names and Attributes that has been mentioned in the Qur'an and the Sunnah of the Prophet ***(SallAllahu alaihi wa sallam)*** while negating that which Allah and His messenger ***(SallAllahu alaihi wa sallam)*** have negated from Allah.

Allah says,

لَيْسَ كَمِثْلِهِ شَيْءٌ وَهُوَ السَّمِيعُ الْبَصِيرُ

"There is nothing like unto Him, and He is the All Hearer, the All Seer." [Surah Ash Shura: 11]

Review Questions

1. What is the meaning of Tawheed?

____

____

2. What is the first category of Tawheed along with its proof?

____

____

____

____

3. What is the second category of Tawheed along with its proof?

____

____

____

____

4. What is the last category of Tawheed along with its proof?

____

____

____

____

____

5. Draw a diagram showing the categories of Tawheed.

❁ ❁ ❁

The Five Pillars of Islaam

The Messenger of Allah *(SallAllahu alaihi wa sallam)* said,

عن أبي عبد الرحمن عبد الله بن عمر بن الخطاب رضي الله عنهما قال:سمعت رسول الله ﷺ يقول: بُني الإسلام على خمس: شهادة أن لا إله إلاَّ الله، وأنَّ محمداً رسول الله، وإقام الصلاة، وإيتاء الزكاة، وحجِّ البيت، وصوم رمضان رواه البخاري ومسلم

"Islam is build on five: The Shahaadah (declaration of faith) That none has the right to be worshipped in truth except Allah and that Muhammad is His slave and messenger, the establishment of prayer (salaat), payment of Zakaah (alms), Hajj (pilgrimage) to the house (i.e. Ka'bah) and Sawm (fast) the month of Ramadhan."

[Collected by Al Bukhaari and Muslim]

Islaam is built of five pillars (Arkan)

1. **The Shahaadah** –This is to testify that none has the right to be worshipped in truth except Allah and that Muhammad *(SallAllahu alaihi wa sallam)* is the Messenger of Allah.

أشهد أن لا إله إلاّ الله

و أشهد أنَّ محمداً رسول الله

(Ash hadu an la ilaha illAllah wa ash hadu ana Muhammadur RasullAllah)

This declaration is what enters one into Islaam. It is a statement of the tongue and an action of the heart.

2. **To establish the Prayer**-It is obligatory on every Muslim to pray the five daily prayers. The daily prayers are 1-Fajr, 2-Dhuhr, 3-Asr, 4-Maghrib, and 5-Isha. Each prayer has a set time and a set unit of rakaat.

   The Prophet *(SallAllahu alaihi wa sallam)* said:

   "Between a man and kufr (disbelief) and shirk, is the leaving of the prayer."

   [Collected by Muslim]

3. **<u>To pay the Zakaah</u>**-This is the yearly charity that the rich Muslims are obligated to pay at the end of the year. This money is paid by the rich and given to the poor.

   Zakaah becomes obligatory if the following conditions are met.

   - When the money reaches the amount of nisaab.

   <u>Nisaab:</u> is the amount of money that if reached makes obligatory the payment of Zakaah.

   <u>The amount of Nisaab:</u> is that which is equal to 84.72 grams of gold or 595 grams of silver.

   - It has to be from the surplus of money (above that which is used for an individuals needs). If he does not have any surplus money because all of it is reserved for his basic needs like: food, drink, clothing, housing, things needed to practice the religion, or marriage; then Zakaah is not obligated upon him.

- The surplus money has to sit for one Islamic year (Hijri) untouched. Meaning the surplus of money that has reached the amount of nisaab that sits for one year without decreasing.
- The money has to have been earned by halaal means (i.e. money that is not earned by illegal acts (i.e. selling of drugs, alcohol, pork, music, or interest from prohibited bank accounts etc...).

The amount of Zakaah: It is approximately 2.5% from ones wealth.

4. **Hajj to the House (Ka'bah)**- Hajj is the pilgrimage that a Muslim must make at least once in his life if he has the ability (financially and health wise). This pilgrimage is made to Mecca and Medinah. The Ka'bah is located in Mecca and the Prophets Masjid is located in Medinah. The reward for the Hajj that is accepted is that one will have all of his sins removed.

The Prophet *(SallAllahu alaihi wa sallam)* said,

"Whoever makes Hajj and does not commit lewd acts nor act sinfully will return just like when his mother gave birth to him (sinless)."

[Collected by Al Bukhaari and Muslim]

5. **<u>To fast the Month of Ramadhan</u>**- A Muslim must fast the month of Ramadhan. Ramadhan is the 9th Month of the Islaamic calendar. A Muslim fasts from Fajr until Maghrib, or in other words from sunrise to sunset. A Muslim leaves off his food, drink, and marital relations for Allah. Ramadhan begins and ends when the new moon is sighted thus alerting the Muslims that a new month has begun if there is an overcast which does not allow the new moon to be seen then the month will end once it has reached thirty days (an Islaamic month is either 29 or 30 days). The reward for fasting this entire month is to have your previous sins forgiven.

The Messenger of Allah *(SallAllahu alaihi wa sallam)* said,

"Whoever fast the month of Ramadhan out of Emaan (faith) and the anticipation of being rewarded Allah would forgive his previous sins."

[Collected by Al Bukhaari]

❁ ❁ ❁

Review Questions

1. How many pillars does Islaam have (provide proof)?

2. What is the Declaration of Faith?

3. Is the Declaration of Faith just a statement on the tongue?

4. How many times a day does a Muslim have to pray?

____

5. What are the names of the prayers?

____

____

6. What did the Prophet *(SallAllahu alaihi wa sallam)* say about the prayer?

____

____

7. What is Zakaah?

____

____

____

____

8. What is the meaning of nisaab?

9. Does the money have to be halal?

10. What is the amount of Zakaah that has to be paid?

11. What is the Hajj?

12. What is the reward for the one whom makes Hajj (provide proof)?

❀ ❀ ❀

The Six Articles of Faith

There are Six Articles of Faith that every Muslim male and female must believe in and affirm.

1. To believe in Allah.
2. To believe in His Angels.
3. To believe in His Books (revealed by Allah).
4. To believe in His Messengers.
5. To believe in the Last Day.
6. To believe in the Qadr (preordainments), the good and the bad of it.

The proof for this is Allah's saying,

لَّيْسَ الْبِرَّ أَن تُوَلُّواْ وُجُوهَكُمْ قِبَلَ الْمَشْرِقِ وَالْمَغْرِبِ وَلَـكِنَّ الْبِرَّ مَنْ آمَنَ بِاللّهِ وَالْيَوْمِ الآخِرِ وَالْمَلآئِكَةِ وَالْكِتَابِ وَالنَّبِيِّينَ

"It is not Al-Birr (piety, righteousness, and every act of obedience to Allah) that you turn your faces towards east and (or) west (in prayers); but al Birr is (the quality of) the one who believes in Allah, the Last Day, the Angels, the Book, the Prophets..." [Surah al Baqarah: 177]

And Allah's saying,

إِنَّا كُلَّ شَيْءٍ خَلَقْنَاهُ بِقَدَرٍ

"Verily, We have created all things with Qadr (Divine Preordainments of all things before their creation as written in the Book of Decrees-Al Lauh Al Mahfuth)." [Surah Qamar: 49]

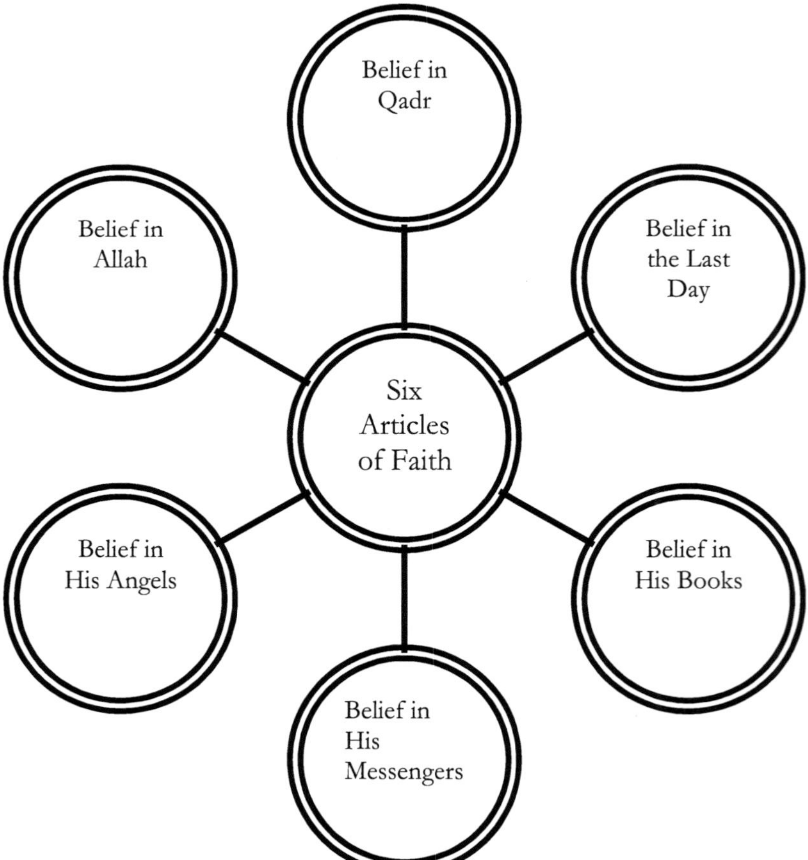

❁ ❁ ❁

Review Questions

1. What are the Six Articles of Faith?

2. What is the proof for the Six Articles of Faith?

3. Draw a diagram of the six Articles of Faith.

❀ ❀ ❀

Ihsan

Ihsan is a pillar alone by itself. Ihsan is to worship Allah as though you see him understanding that you cannot see Him, knowing that He sees you.

Allah says,

إِنَّ اللّٰهَ مَعَ الَّذِينَ اتَّقَوا۟ وَّالَّذِينَ هُم مُّحْسِنُونَ

"Truly, Allah is with those who fear Him (keep their duty unto Him), and those who are Muhsinun (good-doers- those who perform good deeds totally for Allah's sake). [Surah An Nahl: 128]

❁ ❁ ❁

Review Questions

1. What is Ihsan?

2. What is the ayah that mentions the Muhsinun?

Shurootus Salaat

(Conditions of the Salaat)

The conditions of the salaat are nine. These conditions must be met in order for your prayer to be accepted.

1. Al Islaam- The first condition is to be Muslim. Only the salaat of the Muslim is accepted.

   Allah says,

   وَقَدِمْنَا إِلَى مَا عَمِلُوا مِنْ عَمَلٍ فَجَعَلْنَاهُ هَبَاءً مَّنثُورًا

   "And We shall turn to whatever deeds they (disbelievers, polytheists, and sinners) did, and We shall make such deeds as scattered floating particles of dust."[Surah Al Furqaan: 23]

2. Al Aql- The second condition is to be of sound mind. The worshipper who is going to pray has to have an intellect and cannot be insane.

   The Prophet *(SallAllahu alaihi wa sallam)* said,

   "The pen is lifted from three: the person who is sleeping until he awakes, the insane person

until he becomes sane, and the small child until he comes into puberty."

[Collected by Ibn Majah]

3. The third condition is to reach the age of distinction. The age of distinction is seven years old.

   The Prophet *(SallAllahu alaihi wa sallam)* said,

   "Order your children to pray when they reach the age of seven and beat them about it at the age of ten."

   [Collected by Imaam Ahmad, Abu Dawud, and Hakim]

4. The fourth condition is to make Wudu (purification). It is necessary for the one who goes to the prayer to be in a state of Wudu.

   The Prophet *(SallAllahu alaihi wa sallam)* said,

   "Allah does not accept the prayer of the one who breaks his Wudu until he makes Wudu."

   [Collected by Al Bukhaari and Muslim]

5. The fifth condition is the removal of Najas (impurities). The Muslim is required to remove

impurities from three places, his body, clothes, and the place he is going to pray.
Allah says,

وَثِيَابَكَ فَطَهِّرْ

"And purify your garments!" [Surah Al Muddathir: 4]

6. The sixth condition is to cover ones Awrah (private parts). The awrah for the men is from the naval to the knees. The woman's awrah is her whole body excluding her face and hands.
Allah says,

يَا بَنِي آدَمَ خُذُواْ زِينَتَكُمْ عِندَ كُلِّ مَسْجِدٍ

"O Children of Adam! Take your adornment (cover your awrah wearing clean clothes) while praying…" [Surah Al Araf: 31]

7. The seventh condition is that the Salaat has to be prayed in its correct time. The worshipper has to pray when the time for salaat has come in. For example Fajr has to be prayed when the time of Fajr has come in. You cannot pray Fajr if it has not come in yet.

Allah says,

إِنَّ الصَّلَاةَ كَانَتْ عَلَى الْمُؤْمِنِينَ
كِتَابًا مَّوْقُوتًا

"Verily, As Salat is enjoined on the believers at fixed hours." [Surah An Nisaa: 103]

8. The eighth condition is that you must be facing the Qiblah while you are praying. The direction of the Qiblah is towards the Ka'bah in Mecca.

Allah Ta'ala says,

قَدْ نَرَى تَقَلُّبَ وَجْهِكَ فِي السَّمَاءِ فَلَنُوَلِّيَنَّكَ
قِبْلَةً تَرْضَاهَا فَوَلِّ وَجْهَكَ شَطْرَ الْمَسْجِدِ
الْحَرَامِ وَحَيْثُ مَا كُنتُمْ فَوَلُّواْ وُجُوِهَكُمْ شَطْرَه

"Verily, We have seen the turning of your (Muhammad's) face towards the heaven. Surely, We shall turn you to a Qiblah (prayer direction) that shall please you, so turn your face in the direction of Al Masjid al Haram (at Mecca). And wheresoever you people are,

turn your faces (in prayer) in that direction." [Surah Al Baqarah: 144]

9. The ninth condition is the Niyyah (intention). The worshipper must have the intention to pray the salaat. The intention is in the heart not spoken on the tongue. To articulate the niyyah is a bid'ah.

   The Prophet *(SallAllahu alaihi wa sallam)* said,

   "Verily actions are by intentions and everyone will have what he intended."

   [Collected by Al Bukhaari and Muslim]

❁ ❁ ❁

Review Questions

1. How many conditions for salaat are there?

____

2. Only the salaat of a Muslim is accepted, what is the proof for this?

____

____

____

3. The pen is lifted from three, who are they, and what is the proof?

____

____

____

____

____

____

4. When does a Muslim have to start praying?

5. At what age is a child to be beaten if he doesn't pray? Provide the proof.

6. Is the Wudu a condition for the salaat? Provide the proof.

7. Filth and impurities must be removed from three places, what are they?

____

____

8. What is the awrah of the men?

____

What is the awrah for the woman?

____

9. Can you pray any of the salaat if the time for it has not come in yet? Provide the proof.

____

____

____

____

____

10. In what direction does a Muslim have to pray?

11. What is the ruling on articulating the niyyah?

12. Write all of the conditions for the salaat.

The Wudu

As we discussed in the previous lesson before you pray you must make wudu. Wudu is the way the Muslim purifies himself before approaching the salaat.

The steps for making wudu. Everything is started from the right side first.

1. Wash the hands three times from the finger tips to the wrist, going in between the fingers while washing them

2. To make madmadah (rinsing the mouth) and make istinshaaq (sniffing water up the nose) this is done by putting water in the right hand and while making madmadah you make istinshaaq, after istinshaaq you make istinhaar (blowing the water out of the nose) using the left hand. This step is done three times.

3. Then to wash the face three times.

4. Next wash the arms three times starting from the finger tips up to including the elbows.

5. Next wipe the head from the front to the nape of the neck and then back up to the front. Using this same water wipe the inside and outside of the ears using your pointer finger and the thumb.

6. Finally wash the feet three times going in between each toe with your pinky finger and wash up to the ankles including the heel.

❁ ❁ ❁

Review Questions

Write the steps of the wudu in order.

The Things that Nullify the Wudu

The wudu can be nullified (broken) due to a number of causes. If the wudu is nullified you will have to make a new wudu. These are the things that can nullify the wudu:

1. Urine, feces, and flatulence. Whatever exits the private parts- front and rear nullifies the wudu.

2. To fall asleep, lose consciousness, or going insane nullifies the wudu.

3. To apostate nullifies the wudu.

The proof is the statement of Allah,

وَمَن يَكْفُرْ بِالإِيمَانِ فَقَدْ حَبِطَ عَمَلُهُ

"And whoever denies the faith, then his deeds have become worthless" [Surah al Maidah :5]

4. The eating of camel's meat nullifies the wudu.

The daleel is the hadeeth where a man asked the Messenger of Allah *(SallAllahu alaihi wa sallam)* "Do we make wudu from camels meat?" He *(SallAllahu alaihi wa sallam)* said, "yes". [Collected by Muslim]

❁ ❁ ❁

Review Questions

1. What does a Muslim have to do if they break their wudu?

____

____

2. What are the things that can nullify a person's wudu?

____

____

____

____

____

____

3. Write out the proof (the ayat) that apostating nullifies the wudu.

____

4. Write out the proof (the hadeeth) that camel's meat nullifies the wudu.

❁ ❁ ❁

The Shuroot (conditions) of the Wudu

The wudu has conditions that must be met for the one performing the wudu.

1. They have to be Muslim.

2. They have to be sane.

3. They had to have reached the age of discernment.

4. They have to have the niyyah (intention).

5. They have to have the intention to perform the wudu for the salaat, until he has finished purifying himself.

6. The reason for having to make wudu has stopped, example flatulence, you have to wait to start the wudu until you are finished the act of passing wind.

7. You have to make istinjaa (cleaning the private parts with water) and istijmaar (cleaning the private parts with rocks, leaves, etc...).

8. The water is pure and lawful.

9. You have to remove from yourself anything that would prevent the water from touching the skin (i.e. nail polish).

10. The time for the salaat has come in; this is pertaining to the one who has urinary incontinence and the women who are in a state of istihaadah (irregular bleeding).

❁ ❁ ❁

Review Questions

1. Does the wudu has within it conditions?

____

2. Does the wudu of a non Muslim count?

____

3. What is istinjaa?

____

____

4. What is istijmaar?

____

____

5. Can you use water that is impure?

____

6. For what reasons would one have to wait for the salaat to come in to make wudu?

Arkaanus Salaat (Pillars of the Prayer)

The pillars of the salaat are fourteen.

1. Qiyyam (standing if you are able)

The proof is the statement of Allah,

حَافِظُواْ عَلَى الصَّلَوَاتِ والصَّلاَةِ الْوُسْطَى
وَقُومُواْ لِلّهِ قَانِتِينَ

And stand before Allah with obedience (and do not speak to others during the Salât (prayers). [Al-Baqarah: 238]

2. The opening takbir

3. Reciting of Surah Al Faatihah. Surah Al Faatihah is recited in every raka'ah.

The Prophet *(SallAllahu alaihi wa sallam)* said,

"There is no salat for the one who does not recite The Opening Book (Surah Al Faatihah) and it is the Mother of the Qur'aan."

[Collected by Ahmed, Abu Dawud, and Ibn Majaah]

4. Bowing (Ruku)

5. Rising from the bowing (standing)

6. To make sujood (prostration). Prostration is made with seven body parts touching the ground they are; the forehead, nose, hands, knees, and toes.

The proof is the statement from the Prophet *(SallAllahu alaihi wa sallam)*,

"I have been ordered to prostrate on seven body parts."

[Collected by Al Bukhaari and Muslim]

7. Rising from the prostration

8. The sitting between the two prostrations (jalsa)

9. To have tranquility in performing the pillars of the salaat.

10. To perform all of these pillars in order

The proof is the hadeeth of the Abu Hurairah *(Radi Allahu 'anhu)* he said,

"As we were sitting with the messenger *(SallAllahu alaihi wa sallam)* a man came in and prayed then gave salaams to the messenger, he *(SallAllahu alahi wa sallam)* said : "Go back and pray, for verily you have not prayed, the man went back and prayed three times (the same thing kept happening). The man then said, "By the One who sent you with truth as a prophet, I cannot do it better than this, so teach me." The Messenger ***(SallAllahu alaihi was sallam)* said' "When you stand for the prayer say the takbir, then recite what is easy with you from the Qur'aan, then make ruku until you have tranquility, rise until you are standing, then make sujood until you are tranquil in you sujood, then rise until you are sitting tranquil, then do that for the rest of you salaat."**

[Collected by Al Bukhaari and Muslim]

11. The sitting between the last tashaahud

The Prophet *(SallAllahu alaihi wa sallam)* said,

"If anyone sits in the salaat (For Tashaahud) then say at taheyaatu (the greetings)."

[Collected by Al Bukhaari and Muslim]

12. The final Tashaahud

13. Send salaat on the Messenger *(SallAllahu alaihi wa sallam)*

In a hadeeth narrated by Ibn Masud *(Radi Allahu 'anhu)* he asked,

"How do we send salaat upon you? The Messenger of Allah *(SallAllahu alaihi wa sallam)* said, "Oh Allah, bestow your favor on Muhammad and on the family of Muhammad as you have bestowed you favor on Ibraheem and on the family of Ibraheem."

[Collected by Bukhaari and Muslim]

14. The two tasleems

❀ ❀ ❀

Review Questions

1. How many pillars of salaat are there?

2. What is the proof that you have to recite Surah Al Faatihah in every rakaah?

3. How many body parts are supposed to touch the ground when making sujood? (Write them out)

4. What is the proof that you have to prostrate on these body parts?

5. What is the proof that all of the pillars are to be done in order?

6. How do you send salaat upon the Prophet *(SallAllahu alaihi wa sallam)*?

Tawheed and Fiqh

```
Q H K K C K R O E V I Q O M J C Z S M B
Q Q Y Q X O N A S H I E Q Q J U C F Q Y
L K P Q L Z H O A B P E J F A N S B Y A
J E L T A W U Y L V X F P S Z S I U J X
V J Q K A H Y A Q K N Z U H U H H D I V
W H A Y Y I H O O L U J A N N W G P H T
R A A H N I T S I M O R N I O V G A S A
T Y H D M V T T W O W A O N D B K H V F
C Y S H A H A A D A H Q E H R Q O E N F
B I N D A A S K W R U Q B A Q X K Q K I
I B I S L D H B G H R S R J Z Q O E Q S
Z O T A S A A I E J E R H C A H J G U A
B O S Z I M H R T F B E L Y D I A Z K W
Z B I S M D U A H S N P D T O E E T U A
U U F E C A D B P W I M Y P L R Q D R M
L R D K T M Y A M H B F K U K J U T E S
Z L J F R F S Y A I S T X Y D X V K O A
M M C M W Q G M I M B Q A F W A K X S J
Z Q Q T J C C Y O Q N I I B P A Z B L A
W J L Z H V W L U G A N U C K Z U F G N
```

AQL	NIYYAH	TAWHEED
ASMAWASIFFAT	QIBLAH	ULOOHIYYAH
AWRAH	QIYYAM	WUDU
DUAH	RUBOOBIYYAH	ZAKAAT
HAJJ	RUKU	
IHSAN	SALAAT	
ISLAAM	SAWM	
ISTIHAADAH	SHAHAADAH	
ISTINHAAR	SUJOOD	
ISTINSHAAQ	SUNNAH	
MADMADAH	TAKBIR	
NAJAS	TASHAHUD	

English Translations

```
                    H
                   A T R
                   A I P
                  U Q A V N
                  F W F I Y
                 L M U F F E L
                 A V T O R P S
                N Q F N N E E P F
                W O I O O Y R N M
               F B Y I I I A M H B G
N E V W N A M E S A N D A T T R I B U T E S L Y P R W P I
 A G C F K E G W S Y D S A A P S T A N D I N G O Z V N
  F V Z S T A P T T E K C R C S Y K Q K O F Q W Q T
   M Y P L M S N P R O I A Y I P I H S D R O L E
    F K Z I Q W Q B A L L Q B F O E J E D M N
     M B R L S L D M P C G L O I G E T Z T
      H G Z V Y S R P E C E T W R S C I
       L B T R U R U D T I H I I U O
       I S W P R O S T R A T I O N P
       P A O G Y H G U F O V X F F G
      D T V Q Q G X P   M A G I Y B S H
      J P G A B A M       Q V C R E C Y
     W X V P Y C I          B K T P P Z X
     C W T L D Y              V D E I W Q
    S Q N S D Y                 B J Q H Z F
    V I X C Y                     O T E S K
   X U H Z G                        A M U R E
   R U H X                            P G Y O
  X E U X                               S J I W
  J R                                       C T
```

1. ZAKAAT
2. RUKU
3. SHAHADAH
4. SAWM
5. NAJAS
6. NIYYAH
7. RUBOOBIYYAH
8. AL ASMA WA SIFFAT
9. HALAAL
10. HAJJ
11. SALAAT
12. AWRAH
13. SUJOOD
14. WUDU
15. QIYAAM
16. DUAH
17. ULOOHIYYAH

Test Prep

1. **What is Tawheed?**

   Answer:

   Tawheed is the singling out of Allah alone with all worship. It is the religion of the Prophets that Allah sent to teach mankind.

2. **How many categories of Tawheed are there?**

   Answer:

   There are three categories of Tawheed.

3. **What are the three types of Tawheed?**

   Answer:

   1. Tawheed Ar Ruboobiyyah (The Oneness of Allah's Lordship).

   2. Tawheed Al Uloohiyyah (The Oneness of the worship of Allah).

   3. Tawheed Al Asma wa Siffat (The Oneness of the Names and Attributes of Allah).

4. Where in the Qur'an can the three types of Tawheed be found?

Answer:

Allah's says,

بِسْمِ اللّهِ الرَّحْمَنِ الرَّحِيمِ

"In the name of Allah, the Most Beneficent, the Most Merciful." [Surah al Fatihah: 1]

And also His saying,

رَبُّ السَّمَاوَاتِ وَالْأَرْضِ وَمَا بَيْنَهُمَا فَاعْبُدْهُ
وَاصْطَبِرْ لِعِبَادَتِهِ هَلْ تَعْلَمُ لَهُ سَمِيًّا

"Lord of the heavens and the earth and whatever is between them, so worship Him (alone) and be constant and patient in His worship. Do you know of any who is similar to Him? (of course none is similar or coequal or comparable to him, and He has none as a partner with Him). [There is nothing like unto Him and He is the All Hearer, the All Seer]." [Surah Maryam: 65]

5. What is the meaning of Tawheed Ar Ruboobiyyah?

Answer:

To believe in the Oneness of Allah's Lordship. To believe that Allah is the Creator, the One who provides, the Causer of life and death, and other than that from Lordship.

6. What is the proof for Tawheed Ar Ruboobiyyah?

Answer:

The proof of this is Allah's saying,

الْحَمْدُ لِلَّهِ رَبِّ الْعَالَمِينَ

"All praise and thanks belong to Allah the Lord of the Alamin (all that exists, mankind and jinn)." [Surah Al Fatihah: 2]

7. What is the meaning of Tawheed Al Uloohiyyah?

Answer:

This is to believe that Allah is deserving of all worship and that nothing else should be worshiped along with him. All acts of worship are done solely for Allah. A Muslim's salaat (prayer), du'ah (supplication), slaughtering (of animals), seeking forgiveness, love, hope, fear, and other than that are from acts of worship.

8. What is the proof for Tawheed Al Uloohiyyah?

Answer:

Allah says,

وَمَا خَلَقْتُ الْجِنَّ وَالْإِنسَ إِلَّا لِيَعْبُدُونِ

"And I did not create the Jinn and Mankind except to worship Me (alone)." [Surah Adh Dhariyyat: 56]

9. What is the meaning of Tawheed Al Asma wa Siffat?

Answer:

This is to believe in the oneness of Allah's Names and Attributes. To affirm all of Allah's Names and Attributes that has been mentioned in the Qur'an and the Sunnah of the Prophet *(SallAllahu alaihi wa sallam)* while negating that which Allah and His messenger *(SallAllahu alaihi wa sallam)* have negated from Allah.

10. What is the proof for Tawheed Al Asma wa Siffat?

Answer:

Allah says,

لَيْسَ كَمِثْلِهِ شَيْءٌ وَهُوَ السَّمِيعُ الْبَصِيرُ

"There is nothing like unto Him, and He is the All Hearer, the All Seer." [Surah Ash Shura: 11]

11. What are the five pillars of Islaam?

Answer:

The Messenger of Allah *(SallAllahu alaihi wa sallam)* said,

"Islam is build on five: The Shahaadah (declaration of faith) That none has the right to be worshipped in truth except Allah and that Muhammad is His slave and messenger, the establishment of prayer (salaat), payment of Zakaah (alms), Hajj (pilgrimage) to the house (i.e. Ka'bah) and Sawm (fast) the

month of Ramadhan." [Collected by Al Bukhaari and Muslim]

12. What is the Shahaadah?

Answer:

This is to testify that none has the right to be worshipped in truth except Allah and that Muhammad *(SallAllahu alaihi wa sallam)* is the Messenger of Allah.

أشهد أن لا إله إلاّ الله

و أشهد أنّ محمداً رسول الله

(Ash hadu an la ilaha illAllah wa ash hadu ana Muhammadur RasullAllah)

This declaration is what enters one into Islaam. It is a statement of the tongue and an action of the heart.

13. What does it mean to establish the prayer?

Answer:

It is obligatory upon every Muslim to pray the five daily salaat. The daily prayers are Fajr, Dhuhr,

Asr, Maghrib, and Isha. Each prayer has a set time and a set unit of rakaat.

The Prophet *(SallAllahu alaihi wa Sallam)* said:

"Between a man and kufr (disbelief) and shirk, is the leaving of the prayer." [Collected by Muslim]

14. What is the payment of Zakaah?

Answer:

This is the yearly charity that the rich Muslims are obligated to pay at the end of the year. This money is paid by the rich and given to the poor.

15. When does Zakaah become obligatory to pay?

Answer:

Zakaah becomes obligatory if the following conditions are met.

- When the money reaches the amount of nisaab.
- It has to be from the surplus of money (above that which is used for an individual's needs). If he does not have any surplus

money because all of it is reserved for his basic needs like: food, drink, clothing, housing, things needed to practice the religion, or marriage; then Zakaah is not obligated upon him.

- The surplus money has to sit for one Islamic year (Hijri) untouched. Meaning the surplus of money that has reached the amount of nisaab that sits for one year without decreasing.

- The money has to have been earned by halaal means (i.e. money that is not earned by illegal acts (i.e. selling of drugs, alcohol, pork, music, or interest from prohibited bank accounts etc...).

16. What is the amount of nisaab?

Answer:

The amount of Nisaab: is that which is equal to 84.72 grams of gold or 595 grams of silver.

17. What is the amount of Zakaah?

Answer:

It is approximately 2.5% from ones wealth.

18. What is Hajj and what is the reward for making it?

Answer:

Hajj is the pilgrimage that a Muslim must make at least once in his life if he has the ability (financially and health wise). This pilgrimage is made to Mecca and Medinah. The ka'bah is located in Mecca and the Prophets Masjid is located in Medinah.

The Prophet *(SallAllahu alaihi wa sallam)* said,

"Whoever makes Hajj and does not commit lewd acts nor act sinfully will return just like when his mother gave birth to him (sinless)."[Collected by Al Bukhaari and Muslim]

19. What month is it obligatory for a Muslim to fast?

Answer:

A Muslim must fast the month of Ramadhan. Ramadhan is the 9th Month of the Islaamic calendar.

20. What is the reward for the Muslim that fasts the Month of Ramadhan?

Answer:

The reward for the one who fasts the Month of Ramadhan is to have all of their previous sins forgiven.

The Messenger of Allah ***(SallAllahu alaihi wa sallam)*** said,

"Whoever fast the month of Ramadhan out of Emaan (faith) and the anticipation of being rewarded Allah would forgive his previous sins." [Collected by Al Bukhaari]

21. What are the Six Articles of Faith?

Answer:

1. To believe in Allah.
2. To believe in the Angels.
3. To believe in the Books (revealed by Allah).
4. To believe in the Messengers.
5. To believe in the Last Day.
6. To believe in the Qadr (preordainments), the good and the bad of it.

22. What is the proof for the Six Articles of Faith?

Answer:

The proof for this is Allah's saying,

لَّيْسَ الْبِرَّ أَن تُوَلُّواْ وُجُوهَكُمْ قِبَلَ الْمَشْرِقِ وَالْمَغْرِبِ وَلَكِنَّ الْبِرَّ مَنْ آمَنَ بِاللّهِ وَ الْيَوْمِ الآخِرِ وَالْمَلآئِكَةِ وَالْكِتَابِ وَالنَّبِيِّينَ

"It is not Al-Birr (piety, righteousness, and every act of obedience to Allah) that you turn your faces towards east and (or) west (in prayers); but al Birr is (the quality of) the one who believes in Allah, the Last Day, the

angels, the Book, the Prophets..." [Surah Al Baqarah: 177]

إِنَّا كُلَّ شَيْءٍ خَلَقْنَاهُ بِقَدَرٍ

"Verily, We have created all things with Qadr (Divine Preordainments of all things before their creation as written in the Book of Decrees-Al Lauh Al Mahfuz)." [Surah Qamar: 49]

23. What is Ihsan?

Answer:

Ihsan is to worship Allah as though you see him understanding that you cannot see Him, knowing that He sees you.

24. What is the ayah that mentions the Muhsinun?

Answer:

Allah says,

إِنَّ اللَّهَ مَعَ الَّذِينَ اتَّقَوا وَّالَّذِينَ هُم مُّحْسِنُونَ

"Truly, Allah is with those who fear Him (keep their duty unto Him), and those who are Muhsinun (good-doers- those who perform good deeds totally for Allah's sake).[Surah An Nahl: 128]

25. What is the Shurootus Salaat?

Answer:

The conditions of the salaat are nine. These conditions must be met in order for your prayer to be accepted they are; Al Islaam, Al Aql, the age of distinction, the making of Wudu, removal of Najas, covering the Awrah, the Salaat has to be prayed in its correct time, must face the Qiblah, and the Niyyah.

26. Is the salaat of a kaafir accepted?

Answer:

No, only the salaat of the Muslim is accepted.

Allah says,

وَقَدِمْنَا إِلَى مَا عَمِلُوا مِنْ عَمَلٍ فَجَعَلْنَاهُ هَبَاءً مَّنثُورًا

"And We shall turn to whatever deeds they (disbelievers, polytheists, and sinners) did, and We shall make such deeds as scattered floating particles of dust." [Surah al Furqaan: 23]

27. What does it mean that the Muslim praying must have an aql?

Answer:

The worshipper who is going to pray has to have an intellect and cannot be insane.

The Prophet *(SallAllahu alaihi wa sallam)* said,

"The pen is lifted from three: the person who is sleeping until he awakes, the insane person until he becomes sane, and the small child until he comes into puberty." [Collected by Ibn Majah]

28. What is the age of distinction?

Answer:

The age of distinction is seven years old.

The Prophet *(SallAllahu alaihi wa sallam)* said,

"Order your children to pray when they reach the age of seven and beat them about it at the age of ten."[Collected by Imaam Ahmad, Abu Dawud, and Hakim]

29. Is it necessary for the one who goes to the prayer to be in a state of Wudu?

Answer:

Yes, The Prophet *(SallAllahu alaihi wa sallam)* said,

"Allah does not accept the prayer of the one who breaks his Wudu until he makes Wudu."[Collected by Al Bukhaari and Muslim]

30. What is meant by the removal of najas?

Answer:

The Muslim is required to remove all impurities from three places, his body, clothes, and the place he is going to pray.

Allah says,

وَثِيَابَكَ فَطَهِّرْ

"And purify your garments!" [Surah Al Muddathir: 4]

31. What is considered the awrah for the men and women?

Answer:

The awrah for the men is from the naval to his knees. The woman's awrah is her whole body excluding her face and hands.

Allah says,

يَا بَنِي آدَمَ خُذُواْ زِينَتَكُمْ عِندَ كُلِّ مَسْجِدٍ

"O Children of Adam! Take your adornment (cover your awrah) while praying..." [Surah Al Araf: 31]

32. Does the salaat have to be prayed in its allotted time?

Answer:

Yes, the worshipper has to pray when the time for salaat has come in. For example Fajr has to be prayed when the time of Fajr has come in. You cannot pray Fajr if it has not come in yet.

Allah says,

إِنَّ الصَّلاَةَ كَانَتْ عَلَى الْمُؤْمِنِينَ كِتَابًا مَّوْقُوتًا

"Verily, As Salat is enjoined on the believers at fixed hours." [Surah An Nisaa: 103]

33. What is the direction of the Qiblah?

Answer:

The direction of the Qiblah is towards the Ka'bah in Mecca.

Allah *(Ta'ala)* says,

قَدْ نَرَى تَقَلُّبَ وَجْهِكَ فِي السَّمَاءِ فَلَنُوَلِّيَنَّكَ قِبْلَةً تَرْضَاهَا فَوَلِّ وَجْهَكَ شَطْرَ الْمَسْجِدِ الْحَرَامِ وَحَيْثُ مَا كُنْتُمْ فَوَلُّوا وُجُوهَكُمْ شَطْرَهُ

"Verily, We have seen the turning of your (Muhammad's) face towards the heaven. Surely, We shall turn you to a Qiblah (prayer direction) that shall please you, so turn your face in the direction of Al Masjid al Haram (at Mecca). And wheresoever you people are, turn your faces (in prayer) in that direction." [Surah Al Baqarah: 144]

33. What is the Niyyah?

Answer:

The worshipper must have the intention to pray the salaat. The intention is in the heart not spoken on the tongue. To articulate the niyyah is a bid'ah.

The Prophet *(SallAllahu alaihi wa sallam)* said,

"Verily actions are by intentions and everyone will have what he intended." [Collected by Al Bukhaari and Muslim]

34. What are the steps for making wudu?

Answer:

The steps for making wudu. Everything is started from the right side first.

1. Wash the hands three times from the finger tips to the wrist, going in between the fingers while washing them.

2. To make madmadah (rinsing the mouth) and make istinshaaq (sniffing water up the nose) this is done by putting water in the right hand and while making madmadah you make istinshaaq, after istinshaaq you make istinhaar (blowing the water out of the nose) using the left hand. This step is done three times.

3. Then to wash the face three times.

4. Next wash the arms three times starting from the finger tips up to and the elbows.

5. Next wipe the head from the front to the nape of the neck and then back up to the front. Using this same water wipe the inside and outside of the ears using your pointer finger and the thumb.

6. Finally wash the feet three times going in between each toe with your pinky finger and wash up to the ankles.

35. What does a Muslim have to do if they break their wudu?

Answer:

If the wudu is nullified you will have to make a new wudu.

36. What are the things that can nullify a person's wudu?

Answer:

1. Urine, feces, and flatulence. Whatever exits the private parts- front and rear nullifies the wudu.

2. To fall asleep, lose consciousness, or going insane nullifies the wudu.

3. To apostate nullifies the wudu.

4. The eating of camel's meat nullifies the wudu.

37. What is the proof that apostating nullifies the wudu?

Answer:

The proof is the statement of Allah,

وَمَن يَكْفُرْ بِالإِيمَانِ فَقَدْ حَبِطَ عَمَلُهُ

"And whoever denies the faith, then his deeds have become worthless" [Surah Al Maidah: 5]

38. What is the proof that camel's meat nullifies the wudu?

Answer:

The daleel is the hadeeth where a man asked the Messenger of Allah *(SallAllahu alaihi wa sallam)*,

"Do we make wudu from camels meat?" He *(SallAllahu alaihi wa sallam)* said, "yes." [Collected by Muslim]

39. What are the shuroot of wudu?

Answer:

1. They have to be Muslim.

2. They have to be sane.

3. They had to have reached the age of discernment.

4. They have to have the niyyah (intention).

5. They have to have the intention to perform the wudu for the salaat, until he has finished purifying himself.

6. The reason for having to make wudu has stopped, example flatulence, you have to wait to start the wudu until you are finished the act of passing wind.

7. You have to make istinjaa (cleaning the private parts with water) and istijmaar (cleaning the private parts with rocks, leaves, etc...).

8. The water is pure and lawful.

9. You have to remove from yourself anything that would prevent the water from touching the skin (i.e. nail polish).

10. The time for the salaat has come in; this is pertaining to the one who has urinary

incontinence and the women who is in a state of istihaadah (irregular bleeding).

40. How many pillars of salaat are there?

Answer:

The pillars of the salaat are fourteen.

41. What are the Arkanus Salaat?

Answer:

1. Qiyyam (standing if you are able)
2. The opening takbir
3. Reciting of surah al Fatihah. Surah al Fatihah is recited in every raka'ah.
4. Bowing (Ruku)
5. Rising from the bowing (standing)
6. To make sujood (prostration). Prostration is made with seven body parts touching the ground they are; the forehead, nose, hands, knees, and toes.
7. Rising from the prostration

8. The sitting between the two prostrations (jalsa)

9. To have tranquility in performing the pillars of the salaat.

10. To perform all of these pillars in order

11. The sitting between the last tashaahud

12. The final Tashaahud

13. Send salaat on the Messenger *(SallAllahu alaihi wa sallam)*

14. The two tasleems

42. What is the proof that you have to recite Surah Al Fatihah in every rakaah?

Answer:

The Prophet *(SallAllahu alaihi wa sallam)* said,

"There is no salat for the one who does not recite The Opening Book (Surah Al Fatihah) and it is the Mother of the Qur'aan. [Collected by Ahmed, Abu Dawud, and Ibn Majaah]

43. What is the proof that you must prostrate with the seven body parts touching the ground?

Answer:

The proof is the statement from the Prophet *(SallAllahu alaihi wa sallam)*,

"I have been ordered to prostrate on seven body parts." [Collected by Al Bukhaari and Muslim]

44. What is the proof that all of the pillars are to be done in order?

Answer:

The proof is the hadeeth of the Abu Hurairah *(radi Allahu 'anhu)* he said,

"As we were sitting with the messenger *(SallAllahu alaihi wa sallam)* a man came in and prayed then gave salaams to the messenger, he *(SallAllahu alaihi wa sallam)* said : "Go back and pray, for verily you have not prayed, the man went back and prayed three times (the same thing kept happening). The man then said, "By the One who sent you with truth as a prophet, I cannot do it better than this, so teach me." The Messenger *(SallAllahu alaihi*

was sallam) **said' "When you stand for the prayer say the takbir, then recite what is easy with you from the Qur'aan, then make ruku until you have tranquility, rise until you are standing, then make sujood until are tranquil in you sujood, then rise until you are sitting tranquil, then do that for the rest of you salaat." [Collected by Al Bukhaari and Muslim]**

45. How do you send salaat upon the Prophet *(SallAllahu alaihi wa sallam)*?

Answer:

In a hadeeth narrated by Ibn Masud *(radi Allahu 'anhu)* he asked,

"How do we send salaat upon you? The Messenger of Allah *(SallAllahu alaihi wa sallam)* said, "Oh Allah, bestow your favor on Muhammad and on the family of Muhammad as you have bestowed you favor on Ibraheem and on the family of Ibraheem." [Collected by Bukhaari and Muslim]

❀ ❀ ❀